Dear Parents:

Congratulations! Your child is taking the first steps on an exciting journey. The destination? Independent reading!

STEP INTO READING® will help your child get there. The program offers five steps to reading success. Each step includes fun stories and colorful art or photographs. In addition to original fiction and books with favorite characters, there are Step into Reading Non-Fiction Readers, Phonics Readers and Boxed Sets, Sticker Readers, and Comic Readers—a complete literacy program with something to interest every child.

Learning to Read, Step by Step!

Ready to Read   Preschool–Kindergarten
• big type and easy words • rhyme and rhythm • picture clues
For children who know the alphabet and are eager to begin reading.

Reading with Help   Preschool–Grade 1
• basic vocabulary • short sentences • simple stories
For children who recognize familiar words and sound out new words with help.

Reading on Your Own   Grades 1–3
• engaging characters • easy-to-follow plots • popular topics
For children who are ready to read on their own.

Reading Paragraphs   Grades 2–3
• challenging vocabulary • short paragraphs • exciting stories
For newly independent readers who read simple sentences with confidence.

Ready for Chapters   Grades 2–4
• chapters • longer paragraphs • full-color art
For children who want to take the plunge into chapter books but still like colorful pictures.

STEP INTO READING® is designed to give every child a successful reading experience. The grade levels are only guides; children will progress through the steps at their own speed, developing confidence in their reading.

Remember, a lifetime love of reading starts with a single step!

Visit us on the Web!
StepIntoReading.com
rhcbooks.com

Educators and librarians, for a variety of teaching tools, visit us at RHTeachersLibrarians.com

ISBN 978-1-5247-6799-0 (trade) — ISBN 978-1-5247-6800-3 (lib. bdg.)

Printed in the United States of America   10 9 8 7 6 5 4 3 2 1

Happy Birthday to You!

by Kristen L. Depken
illustrated by Dave Aikins

Random House 🏠 New York

4

Shimmer and Shine
are throwing
a birthday party!
Who is it for?

Shimmer makes
a cake.

It is not her birthday.

8

Shine hangs
streamers.

It is not her birthday.

Tala puts on music.
Is it her birthday?
No.

Nahal blows up balloons.

It is not her birthday.

13

It is party time!
Leah comes
to the palace.

Is she
the birthday girl?
No.

Zac comes, too.
Is he
the birthday boy?
No.

Shimmer sets up

a birthday game.

Shine puts out
the birthday presents.

What a fun party!
But who is it for?

20

Surprise!

The party is for <u>you</u>!

23

Happy birthday to you!